JUSTICE, MY LORD!

Stewart Ross

CONTENTS

TO THE READER

Justice, My Lord! is about Magna Carta (the Great Charter), one of the most important documents ever produced. It explains, in the form of an exciting story, how and why it was written. All the main facts in the story are true, and the de Mowbrays, King John and Bishop Hugh really existed. I have made up a few details in order to bring to life to one of the most dramatic episodes in our history.

Stewart Ross

THE STORY SO FAR ...

Henry II ruled England from 1154 to 1189. His marriage to Eleanor of Aquitaine, a great landowner, made him one of the most powerful men in all Europe. But when the quickest means of communication was on horseback, it was almost impossible to manage lands that stretched from Scotland to the Pyrenees. Moreover, many great lords, known as barons, were jealous of Henry's wealth and power, and he faced several rebellions.

Part of the problem was that no one knew exactly what a king was and was not allowed to do. Could he make up the law, for example, and could he ask people to pay any tax he demanded? Probably not. Sensible kings always discussed such matters with their family and with the barons.

When Henry II died, his son Richard inherited the crown. Known as the Lionheart, Richard was a warrior king. He spent much of his reign (1189-1199) fighting on a crusade in the Holy Land and battling to hang on to his lands in France. He spent only a few months in England.

Richard had no children. This left his brother John next in line for the throne. When Richard was away, John had rebelled and tried to seize the kingdom. He failed, and Richard forgave him for his treachery. But such behaviour gave John a bad reputation. So, when

Richard was killed and John took up the crown, many feared grim times lay ahead.

TIME LINE

CE (Common Era)

1100

Henry I becomes King. He issues a Charter of Liberties stating that the King has to obey the law.

1167

John, future King of England, born..

c.1173

William de Mowbray born.

1193

John rebels against his brother, Richard I.

1204

John loses most of his lands in France.

1203

Arthur of Brittany disappears, believed murdered by John.

1199

Death of Richard I. John becomes King.

1189

Richard I (the Lionheart) becomes King.

c.1176

Avice Daubigny, future wife of William de Mowbray, born.

1154-1189

Reign of Henry II, father of Richard I and John.

1000

1208

John begins a quarrel with the Pope.

1213

William de Mowbray and other barons refuse to serve
with John's army in France. John's allies are defeated.

1215

Barons draw up a long charter of demands.
It is based on Henry I's Charter of Liberties.
John sets his seal on the barons' Great
Charter (Magna Carta).

2015

Worldwide celebrations
mark the 800th
anniversary of Magna
Carta.

c.1224

Death of William de Mowbray.

2015

1297

Magna Carta becomes
English law.

1687

Magna Carta printed
in America.

1216

Death of King John.

1214

Barons launch an armed
rebellion against the King.

1628

King Charles I accepts the
Petition of Right, a document
that quotes Magna Carta.

1212

John's money-raising has made him wealthy –
but highly unpopular. Revolts against his rule begin.

Chapter 1

LADY AVICE'S STORY

I was just setting down for my afternoon nap when I was roused by a fearful hammering at my front door. 'Father Robin!' cried a voice. 'Father Robin, you're wanted!'

I hauled myself to my feet, crossed to the door and opened it. The July sunlight streamed in, blinding me for a moment. I blinked and looked down at my visitor.

I say 'down' because the person making all that din was little Tom Ketch, the nine-year-old servant from the manor. The lad's mother and father had died that spring. When I told Lady Avice that the poor orphan boy had no relations and would shortly die of starvation, she took pity on him and let him join her household.

She's like that, Lady Avice. A good woman.

Anyway, Tom was all of a fluster. I was needed at Epworth Manor immediately, he panted. 'Come like you was chased by a bull,' he said. 'Her Ladyship says as she is in need of you something urgent, father.'

I didn't ask what the hurry was because I didn't need to. Lady Avice had not been in good health for a while now, not since the death of her husband. *Obviously*, I told myself, *she is dying, and she needs me to be there at the moment of her passing.*

I was wrong. Or, to be more accurate, I was half wrong.

When I arrived at the manor, I found Her Ladyship sitting in her parlour surrounded by half-a-dozen servants. She looked pale and frail, but certainly not about to die.

'Lady Avice,' I said as I entered the room, 'I am come.'

'Tsh! I can see that, Father Robin. Now sit down at that table over there – yes, the one with the ink and parchment on it – and do as I say.'

I did as I was told. Her Ladyship was not the sort of person to argue with. As I was settling myself down, she gave Tom a small coin and sent him out of the room together with the other servants.

'Right, Father Robin,' she began as soon as we were alone, 'now I can tell you why I sent for you. You know how to write, I assume?'

I told her I did, and I was very proud of my handwriting.

'Good. And I can trust you to keep a secret?'

'Of course, Your Ladyship.'

'Well, let us begin. As you know, I am very old and will soon be dead.'

At this, I opened my mouth to object, but she waved a thin hand and said sharply, 'Don't be foolish, Father Robin. There's no point in pretending. Both of us know I won't see another Christmas.

'But before I go, I want to set the record straight.'

'The record, My Lady?'

'Yes. I want the world to know the truth about my husband. There are those who say he was a wicked man, a rebel and an ungodly sinner. Lies, all lies! And you know who spread them?'

'No, My Lady, I do not.' That wasn't strictly true. I had a fairly good idea, but I didn't dare mention his name.

Lady Avice saw through this at once. 'Ah! Coward! But I don't blame you. Kings can always hurt you, even from the grave. But I'm beyond caring.

'John. King John, John Lackland, John Softsword – give him any name you want, it's still the same devil. He's the villain who blackened my William's name with his foul lies.

'But now's the time for truth, so write it down as I tell you.'

I nodded and dipped my quill in the ink. What follows is the story of Lady Avice de Mowbray, word for word, exactly as she dictated it to me.

Chapter 2

SO SMALL!

Even before he became King, John was laughing at my husband and spreading stories about him. I got to hear of them and, though we weren't married then, they struck me as a bit harsh.

While still in his teens, William had gone off to the Holy Land to fight with Richard the Lionheart. As you know, Richard was a giant of a man. According to William, he was almost six-and-a-half feet tall and as broad as an ox – every inch a warrior king.

My William was the opposite, a warrior in miniature. He was scarcely five feet tall. Prince John called him and Richard "the elephant and the lamb". He sniggered and made baa-baa noises whenever the name of William de Mowbray was mentioned. His friends smiled, but I believe they were more embarrassed than amused. King Richard would never have stooped to such low, bullying behaviour. William said the King never once mentioned his size to him. Instead, he was full of praise for William's bravery and honour.

I think William really loved Richard. He used to call him the "perfect knight in every way". He would have done anything for him: that's why he stayed with him for two years when he was taken hostage on the way back from the Holy Land.

William's hero-worship of Richard was the main reason why John hated him. You see, John couldn't stand his elder brother, so anyone close to Richard was automatically an enemy of John. That was alright as long as Richard was alive and still King, but when he died and John took over the crown, my William was in trouble.

William and I were married shortly after he came back to this country. I've now got a confession to make. When my mother first told me I was to marry Sir William de Mowbray, I almost had a fit.

'Mother!' I cried. 'How could you even think of marrying me to that, that...' I was so upset I couldn't even think of the word.

'Yes? What's the matter with him, Avice? The de Mowbray family is as good as the Daubignys. You're distant cousins, in fact. And he's a brave knight who has fought with the King.'

'I know, I know,' I said, tears welling up in my eyes. 'But he's so *small*!'

My mother smiled. 'Remember, Avice, that David defeated Goliath. Anyway, small or not, he's the husband we've chosen for you. And when you've got over your silly crying, I don't think you'll be disappointed.'
She was right.

We saw each other for the first time when he came to our castle at Arundel to ask for my hand. It was all a show, of course, because our parents had arranged the marriage long before. But at least we had a chance to get to know each other before we became husband and wife.

My first reaction was, 'Oh no! He's even tinier than they said he was!' And then he smiled at me. When some people smile their mouths move, but that's all. You can see in their eyes they are not smiling inside. King John was like that – but not William de Mowbray.

When my William smiled his whole face blazed like a fire in the great hall, throwing out light and warmth to everyone around. After chatting to him for a short time, I no longer noticed how much taller than him I was. It didn't matter. We were already the best of friends – and remained so for the rest of our lives.

One of the things I most appreciated about William was how he shared everything with me. I think he realised that I'm quite smart, and it didn't take him long to see that when there's a problem, two heads are better than one.

You can guess what this meant, can't you? As the wife and close friend of William de Mowbray, I joined my husband in Prince John's black book. I'm told he laughed when he heard of our marriage. 'The Lady Avice must be a feeble donkey,' he scoffed, 'marrying only half a man.'

From that moment on, I hated him.

Chapter 3

REVENGE

When we were married, William was lord of lands in France and England. This meant he was away a lot. I missed his company, of course, but I kept myself busy looking after our estates in Yorkshire and Lincolnshire.

This was when our children were born: Nigel, Alice, Katherine and little Avice. William insisted on my name for our youngest daughter. He said the word "Avice", like me, was special and should be passed on.

The news of King Richard's death came as an unpleasant shock. He was only 41 and in good health. But soldiers live dangerously, and I should not have been surprised to hear he had been hit by an arrow, and that poison from the wound had spread swiftly around his body.

You know, I suppose, that Richard forgave the archer who fired that arrow? It was typical of the man – generous to the last. The same could certainly not be said of his mean-minded successor.

John had always wanted the crown. He even tried to seize it when his brother was away on crusade. The rebellion did not come to much: hardly anyone was prepared to support someone trying to rob a crusader fighting for Christ in the Holy Land. Good people just don't do that sort of thing. But, as I've said, John was not a good man.

I discovered this for myself the first time we met. Even now, all these years later, I still quiver with anger when I think of it. The new king was in York and he summoned all the local barons to meet him there. 'And bring your wives,' he leered. 'We'll have a little dancing.'

I'll give John one thing: he knew how to throw a party. The great hall of the castle was brilliant with flags and tapestries. Minstrels sang, poets recited their verses, and the table groaned with delicious dishes. And in the midst of all this splendour, like a smooth-skinned toad, sat King John.

The moment he spoke to me I knew what he was up to. Though he was married, he had a reputation for chasing other women. William had warned me of this, so I knew what to expect.

'Ah, the delightful Lady Avice,' he smirked, running his eyes over me as if I were a horse he was thinking of buying. 'You are even more beautiful than I have heard say.'

That was a lie for a start. I know I'm not beautiful. My skin is too rough, and my dull brown eyes are set too far apart. Besides, I'm short-sighted, which makes me frown. Flattery would get the King nowhere.

When he asked to meet me later so he could show me some piece of needlework he had just bought, I refused. 'Very well,' he scowled. 'Suit yourself.'

With that, he lost interest in me. But he did not forget the incident, and soon afterwards he took a cruel and greedy revenge.

I need to fill you in with a bit of de Mowbray family history.

During the reign of King Henry I, his brother Robert, nicknamed "Shortypants", tried to steal the crown. One of the barons who backed Shortypants was a nasty piece of work named Destuteville. Anyway, the Shortypants rebellion failed, and Henry handed out the rebels' estates to those who had stuck by him. He gave some of the Destuteville land to the de Mowbrays. End of story.

Except it wasn't the end of the story. As soon as John became king, William Destuteville complained to him that his family estates had been given away unjustly. He wanted them back. I don't think John could have cared less who had the lands; but whenever there was a quarrel between barons, his eyes lit up. Settling a dispute was an opportunity to make money.

William and I knew this. Immediately after we heard what Destuteville was up to, we sat down to work out what to do.

'One thing's for certain,' frowned William. 'The King won't make a decision based on what's right. Oh no! He'll decide who he likes best and who'll pay him the most money.

'Which means, Avice my love, that we're about to get a whole lot poorer.'

Chapter 4

JACOB OF LINCOLN

William called a meeting of the stewards from his estates on both sides of the Channel. It took a while, but in the end they worked out that, when the harvest was good, he had an income of about 500 marks a year.

'Will that be enough to give the King?' I asked.

William shook his head. 'Afraid not, Avice.'

'Double it?'

'Double it again, and we may be getting close.'

'What?' I cried. 'That's 2,000 marks! We'll never be able to raise that much.'

William agreed. 'There's only one answer. We'll have to borrow it.'

'The priests say borrowing money is wrong,' I said.

'I know,' William sighed. 'But I'm afraid we don't have much choice.'

We were both from baronial families. We knew about dancing, hunting and fighting, but almost nothing about business. Money matters were for merchants, not nobles. We needed advice.

The man we turned to was Bayard, the quick-witted steward of our estates on the Isle of Axholme. Before working for us, he had travelled widely and picked up all sorts of tips about how business worked.

Yes, he said, he knew where to get hold of money.

We could either go to one of the Italian bankers who had recently set up in London, or we could use a local man.

Which did he recommend?

Bayard said a local man would be best, and he knew an honest and reliable moneylender with offices in Lincoln. His name was Jacob, and if we agreed, he'd ride over to the city and invite him to come and meet us.

And so, a week later, we found ourselves sitting at the table in the great hall with Bayard on one side and Jacob the moneylender on the other. The steward explained we needed a loan of 2,000 marks.

Jacob sucked in air through his teeth and looked at William. 'Two thousand, My Lord? That's a huge sum. I'm not sure –'

'Oh come on, Jacob!' chuckled Bayard. 'Of course you can find it. You needn't worry about getting repaid, either. As I'm sure you know, the de Mowbrays have estates all over England and Normandy. They just need a little immediate cash, that's all.'

'A little immediate cash,' said Jacob wryly. 'Well, it can be done. But there will be a charge, of course. As you are an honourable man, Baron de Mowbray, I will ask for only 22 percent interest per year. That's... Let me see...' He paused and stared at the ceiling for a moment. 'Yes, that's 19 pence and the odd farthing per day.'

They were terrifying figures, but there was no alternative if we were to buy the King's support against that double-dealing Destuteville. With Bayard's help, an agreement was drawn up and signed by William and Jacob. My husband then set off for London to tell John of the generous gift we had for him.

* * *

I didn't go to London myself, but William told me what happened. John was delighted to hear how much he was being offered. 'Two thousand marks!' he exclaimed. 'That's most kind of you, Lord Mowbray. It looks as if I was wrong about you. You're not such a bad fellow after all, are you?'

William did not reply. He bowed low and left the hall. But before the doors shut behind him, he heard the King say, 'Ah! Destuteville! I wonder what you have come to see me about?'

William's heart sank. He had agreed to hand over all that money but had received nothing definite in return. *Typical of that snake of a king*! he thought.

Two weeks later a royal messenger arrived. The quarrel over lands between Baron William de Mowbray and Sir William Destuteville would be settled by the Bishop of Lincoln, he announced. Both sides were required to meet at the Bishop's palace five days after Whitsun.

When William heard this, he used language that even now makes me blush.

Chapter 5

THE BISHOP

This time I decided to go with William. Not that I didn't trust him. Rather, as I said before, we worked better when we were together.

It rained all the way from our manor at Axholme to Lincoln. The roads were flooded, and by the time I arrived I was covered in mud from head to toe. We stayed just outside the city with a relative of William's, Hugh Depatri. He had a large manor with plenty of room for our servants and stabling for our horses. By the time we had changed our clothes and had a good meal, we felt ready for anything – even a meeting with the saintly Bishop of Lincoln.

Hugh of Avalon, Bishop of Lincoln, was famous for being especially holy. He came from a noble French family and had spent his early years as a monk. If anyone was going to give a fair judgement in our case, it should have been him. But it wasn't.

We got a clue to what might happen even before we entered the city. As we drew near, we looked up at the famous cathedral. Something was wrong. It was covered in wooden scaffolding, and parts of it looked as if they had recently fallen down.

When we asked what was going on, we were told that five years ago the cathedral had been badly damaged by an earthquake. Bishop Hugh was now rebuilding it bigger and more beautiful than ever.

'In other words,' I whispered to William, 'he needs money.'

We met our second problem in the entrance hall of the bishop's palace. His secretary took one look at me and shook his head. 'I am very sorry, My Lady, but his Grace will not hold a conversation with women.'

'I beg your pardon?' said William angrily. 'This is no ordinary woman. This is my wife, the Lady Avice de Mowbray. Where I go, she goes.'

The secretary made a tutting noise. 'Except here, My Lord. His Grace has given very specific instructions: no women. They are, he says, a distraction.'

'A distraction! Our Lord Jesus Christ spent his life surrounded by women...'

It was no use. Whatever William said, the secretary would not change his mind, and I ended up waiting on a hard bench outside the meeting room. When the discussions were over, William told me what had gone on. It did not make pleasant listening.

The moment William entered the bleak chamber where Bishop Hugh was seated, he sensed there were going to be difficulties. His Grace was charming and polite – but seemed to live in a totally different world.

'Land?' he said after the case had been explained to him. 'My dear de Mowbray and Destuteville, what is land? It is a source of wealth. And what is wealth? It is sent by the devil to tempt us from the path of holiness.

'It is easier,' he went on, 'for a camel to pass through the eye of a needle than for a rich man to enter the Kingdom of Heaven.'

He looked at William. 'You wish to enter the Kingdom of Heaven, Baron de Mowbray?'

'Indeed I do, Your Grace.'

'And you, Destuteville?'

Instead of replying immediately, the wily fox fell to his knees. 'Oh yes!' he cried. 'Save my soul, please Your Grace. I care nothing for land or wealth. If by God's mercy I were to regain the lands stolen from our family, I will give half – no, three-quarters – of the income to you, Your Grace, for rebuilding God's holy cathedral.'

Hearing this, Bishop Hugh appeared to go into a sort of trance. He muttered to no one in particular, 'Your money plus the King's reward for my judgement in this case... A new tower! No, two new towers!'

William realised at once what had happened. King John had accepted money from Destuteville as well as the 2,000 marks from us. While keeping most of this for himself, he had handed over a few hundred to Bishop Hugh for his cathedral fund. It was a bribe – though I'm sure the unworldly bishop didn't realise it – to make sure the judgement went against us.

As a result, John pocketed a fortune; the Bishop got his two towers; Destuteville got the land he wanted (and, incidentally, never paid a penny towards the rebuilding of the cathedral); and we got... Nothing.

Actually, that's not quite true. We had got something:

an enormous debt.

I think, Father Robin, you can now begin to see why my husband, a good man, disliked King John so much. As we rode back to Axholme, he said he hoped that Justice, that most virtuous lady, would one day smile on poor England again.

My William could be quite poetic when the mood took him, couldn't he?

Chapter 6

THIS CANNOT GO ON!

Remember how, when I began my story, I said I wanted to tell you what an honest man my husband was? Well, listen to this.

Do you know what did he do when he learned King John had swindled him out of his lands? Did he rebel, sulk or join up with the armies of the King of France? No, he remained loyal. And not just by saying the right things, either. He actually went to war beside King John in France and in Ireland.

Yes, William de Mowbray risked his life for a man who had cheated him. That's almost saintly.

But there are limits, and as the years went by even William's patience wore thin.

First there was the pathetic fighting in France. When John became king, his estates ran from Scotland to the Pyrenees. Because so few would fight for him, he managed to lose just about the whole lot in four years. Are you surprised he got the nickname "Softsword"?

And it wasn't just the King who suffered. The French seized the de Mowbray lands on the other side of the Channel, too. Now we had fewer estates, we received less rent. So just after we'd taken out a loan of 2,000 marks, we suddenly had far less money to pay it back with. We were not happy, I can tell you.

Many of our friends suffered in the same way. Old Baron Debros, a mighty warrior who had fought beside Henry II and Richard the Lionheart in the Holy Land, was so angry he couldn't bring himself to utter the King's name. Instead of saying "John", he made a gurgling noise in the back of his throat, as if he were being sick!

You should have heard him! 'I will not have King Urgh mentioned in my household,' he used to say. 'That Urgh is the King of Crooks!'

William and I couldn't help laughing, even though such talk was clearly treason.

The business with his nephew, young Arthur of Brittany, damaged John's reputation still further. Because some said the boy was the true king, John murdered him with his own hands. Yes, I know the official story is that Arthur "disappeared", but no one believed it.

I learned the truth a couple of years ago. One night, John got drunk and stabbed the lad. Panicking, he weighed the body down with stones and threw it into the River Seine. A fisherman dredged it up the next day by mistake. He gave it a decent burial, but at the time he was too terrified to tell anyone.

The final straw for us came when John put a new tax on moneylenders...

Jacob appeared at the end of a hot Thursday afternoon in July. A day rather like today, in fact. My husband and I were outside taking a walk in the garden when he approached.

'Baron de Mowbray, Lady de Mowbray,' he said, bowing, 'I hope I find you well.'

'Tolerably so,' replied my husband. 'And you, Jacob, how are things in the world of banking?'

'Very bad, My Lord. Very bad indeed.'

'But the moneylenders of Lincoln haven't been attacked, have they? I haven't heard anything.'

Jacob gave him a suspicious look. 'No attacks on our bodies, My Lord, but on our property.'

'I thought this was coming, Jacob. You're finding it difficult to pay the new tax?'

'Precisely, My Lord.'

'And you want me to repay more of the money I owe you so you can pay the King's unfair tax?'

'More or less, My Lord. Though I did not use the word "unfair".'

'No, of course you didn't. To do so might cost you your life. Therefore I will speak for you.

'Everything this King does is cruel and unfair. He's broken every promise he made to us at his coronation... This cannot go on!'

Chapter 7

JUSTICE, MY LORD!

Everyone we knew had had enough. One of William's old soldier colleagues, Robert Fitzwalter, was so angry that he made plans to kill the king. When we were down in London, he asked William if he'd join the plot. We had a long talk about it, and in the end decided that violence was not the answer.

'It's a matter of John sticking to what he promised when he was crowned,' William said. 'Things like getting our approval before putting up taxes, and using the law courts for justice, not for collecting money.' He was still furious at the way we had been swindled over the Destuteville land.

'What we need,' I said, wishing I had received more education, 'is for someone to write down what the King can and cannot do. Then get him to promise to stick to those rules.'

'John's promises are not worth an apple pip. His word is like a dandelion, blown away by the next breath that comes along.'

'Then you and your friends must keep an eye on him and make sure he keeps his promises.'

'Me? My dearest Avice –'

And that's as far as our conversation went. We were interrupted by Hugh Depatri bursting into our room.

'I'm so sorry to disturb you,' he blurted, 'but have you heard the latest?'

William got to his feet. 'No. What is it?'

'The King...'

William groaned. 'What's he up to this time?'

'He's ordered all his barons and knights to go to France with him. He says he's going to get back all the land he lost.'

William sat down again. 'Not going,' he said, resting the palms of his hands squarely in the arms of his chair. 'Simple as that. Avice and I are returning to Axholme. If the King wants me to go gallivanting over to France with him, he must come and fetch me.'

* * *

After this, each day seemed to bring fresh news and rumours – we were unable to tell one from the other. John had handed over England to the Pope... John's army in France had been utterly defeated... John was bankrupt... John was going on a crusade... John demanded an even higher tax from his barons and knights...

Talk of a yet another tax was the last straw. We sent messages to all our friends who felt as we did it: meet at Stamford on the Great North Road. Come armed and with as many men as you can muster.

William's armourer sharpened up his weapons, the blacksmith re-shoed his horse, and Bayard arranged for all the de Mowbray knights and soldiers to gather at Axholme. It was winter now, and bitterly cold as I stood at the window of the manor to watch William lead his small army south. It was a desperate venture – but we lived in desperate times.

John met the rebels in the Great Hall of Westminster, built by his ancestor, William Rufus. He kept them waiting for a good hour before arriving in a procession that would have done King Solomon proud. Trumpets blared as the royal guards entered, each dressed in silver-edged armour that glinted in the light of a thousand candles. Then came a dozen chanting priests in spotless cassocks, bishops in tall mitre hats, and the Archbishop of Canterbury himself in a golden robe.

Hugh Depatri leaned towards William. 'Posh lot, aren't they?' he whispered.

'Aye. And I wonder who paid for it all, eh?'

John followed the Archbishop. His gaudy royal robes, made specially for the occasion, made him look like a cross between a nun and a jester. When all was ready, he raised his eyes sorrowfully and spoke. He loved us all, he said, and wanted nothing more than peace and harmony throughout his kingdom. He hoped he had done no man wrong.

'What is it you desire of me, dear friends?' he concluded. 'Tell me! And whatever you wish for, I will grant you.'

For a long time no one said a word. William wondered why. Then, looking about, he realised all eyes were fixed on him. *Right*, he thought, *if no one else will say why we're here, I certainly will.*

'We have but one demand,' he said, his voice ringing round the hall. 'One very simple and reasonable demand. It is for justice, My Lord!'

Chapter 8

A GREAT CHARTER

William's speech was followed by a lot of muttering and mumbling as the King discussed with Archbishop Stephen Langton how he should respond. Eventually the royal party said they needed more time to think things over. Would the barons be prepared to leave London and meet again in Northampton in the spring?

Now it was the turn of William and his friends to mutter and mumble. After much debate they accepted the King's suggestion. They would gather in Northampton on 26 April. Shortly afterwards, the meeting broke up and William returned home.

'So what are you going to do now?' I asked when we were alone after dinner.

William placed his hand over mine. 'After our meeting with the King, I asked my friends exactly the same question, Avice.'

'And what did they say?'

'They weren't too sure, so I made a suggestion to them. I told them what you said, about writing down what the King had promised at his coronation, and making him stick to it.'

I felt rather proud that the suggestion of an illiterate woman had been put before all those mighty barons. 'So what did they think of my idea?' I asked.

'They liked it. But unfortunately no one could remember exactly what John *had* promised at his coronation.

'We were rescued by Baron Debros. He said he recalled his great-grandfather talking about a list of promises – it was called a charter – made by the first King Henry at his coronation. If we could find that, he said, we could add new bits and get King John to set his seal on it.'

'And who's supposed to find this charter?'

'I am. But I haven't a clue...'

There was a pause. Our eyes met and, at precisely the same time, we both said, 'Bayard!'

Our faithful steward set off for London the following morning. He had no idea where Henry I's charter was, he confessed, but he knew one or two people who might be able to help.

'Never fear, Lord Mowbray,' he said as he climbed into the saddle. 'I will return with that charter, even if I have to steal it.'

He was as good as his word. Whether he stole the copy of the charter he brought home, we never asked. Actually, I think he copied it. I don't understand writing, but the letters on the charter looked very much like his own. In the end it didn't matter – the barons could now start drawing up a charter of their own.

* * *

As agreed, William and the rebel barons met at Northampton. John did not turn up.

'Typical!' muttered William. 'Well, you can't say we didn't give him a chance. To arms, friends!'

Faced with a country-wide revolt, the King's support melted away like summer hail. He had no choice but to talk. The barons set up a base at Staines and John moved to his castle at Windsor. Through the early summer messages passed back and forth between them until the new charter was ready.

On 15 June, the two sides met in the meadow at Runnymede, beside the River Thames. A clerk produced the document and read it out loud so everyone could hear. It contained all the things William had wanted, including a guarantee of justice and discussions before new taxes were raised.

William and twenty-four other barons would have the job of seeing the charter was obeyed.

John listened to all this with a bored look, yawning and picking at his fingernails. When the clerk had finished, he waved his hand and the royal seal was attached to the bottom of the charter. And that should have been it.

But John, being John, had no intention whatsoever of keeping his word. He broke the terms of the charter almost immediately, and there was little William and his friends could do about it.

But the Great Charter, as it is now known, has not been destroyed. One day, when people are crying out for justice, I'm sure it will be brought out again. And then, perhaps, they will remember my noble husband, William de Mowbray, and quietly thank him for all he did to bring justice to this land.

THE HISTORY FILE

WHAT HAPPENED NEXT?

John

As Lady Avice de Mowbray feared, King John never had any intention of sticking to what was set out in the Great Charter (or Magna Carta in Latin). He attached his seal to it simply to buy time to gather his forces. The rebel barons were furious and soon England was torn by civil war.

The rebels had had enough of John and invited Prince Louis of France to take over the crown. Louis invaded England with a French army and, just when things were looking grim for John, he died (1216). Few people believed he went to Heaven. 'Foul as it is,' wrote one historian at the time, 'Hell is made fouler by the presence of John.'

Henry III

John left a nine-year-old son who was crowned Henry III. The barons gathered round him, the French were driven out and the civil war came to an end. However, as Avice had predicted, Magna Carta was not forgotten. In 1217, it was copied out again (printing had not been invented) with a few changes, and again eight years later. In 1297, when King Edward I needed to increase taxes, Magna Carta became part of the law of the land.

Magna Carta

And the story did not end there. Centuries later, when King Charles I and Parliament were arguing about which of them had the greater authority, Members of Parliament quoted Magna Carta. It showed, they said, that kings had to obey the law. Parliament defeated the King in a civil war and cut off his head (1649). Law – and Magna Carta – had won.

Nowadays, all around the world, people accept that the law is mightier than kings, princes and presidents – an idea that goes back to William de Montfort and Magna Carta.

HOW DO WE KNOW?

King John died over 800 years ago. We sometimes forget exactly what happened last month or last year, so putting together a picture of events many centuries ago is extremely tricky. A few buildings (like Bishop Hugh's cathedral at Lincoln) remain, but they don't give us much information about what people were actually *like*.

To get a fuller picture, historians rely on written sources. Two of the most important are histories written by men living at the time, Roger of Wendover and the Barnwell Chronicler. Roger has hardly a good word to say about John, but the Chronicler speaks quite highly of him. Who was right?

To try to solve such difficulties, historians turn to other sources. Some of the most useful are records of sums of money collected and spent, and of lands bought, sold or given away. Sources like these suggest John really was a mean and grasping king. For example, the story of him taking 2,000 marks from William de Mowbray, and then letting Bishop Hugh give some of William's lands to the Destutevilles, is true. It suggests John was more interested in money than doing the right thing.

And we can still read Magna Carta, perhaps the best source of all. (It's on the internet: www.bl.uk/magna-carta.) The list of things the barons wanted from the King, such as not being sent to prison illegally, give us a fair idea of John's disgraceful behaviour.

NEW WORDS

Archbishop
A chief officer of the Christian church; England has two archbishops, in Canterbury and York

Archer
Person who shoots arrows with a bow

Axholme
Area of Lincolnshire that used to be an island

Bankrupt
Having no money

Baron
Nobleman; a great lord

Bishop
Officer of the church in charge a wide area and many priests

Cassock
Long white robe

Chamber
Large room

Channel
Sea between England and France

Charter
Important document setting out privileges, rights and rules

Civil war
War fought between two groups within the same country

Crusade
War to take back the Holy Land from its Muslim conquerors

Crusader
Christian warrior who fought in the Holy Land

Father
Title given to a priest

Farthing
Coin worth ¼ of an old penny

Holy Land
Land of the Bible: modern-day Israel and Palestine

Grace
Title given to a bishop (eg 'His Grace' and 'Your Grace')